This book belongs to

....

....

www.gwpublishing.com

This is Hamish the haggis
of the McHaggis clan,
never been seen
by the eyes of man.

Hamish

Rupert Harold the Third
is an English gent,
travelling far from
his home in Kent.

Rupert

Our Jeannie's an osprey with wide sweeping wings,
who is easily distracted by all sorts of things.

Jeannie

Angus

Young Angus is cheeky and likes playing the fool.
What ever he's doing, he's got to look cool!

For my Mum
with love. L.S.

For Chris
with love. S.J.C.

Text and Illustrations copyright © Linda Strachan and Sally J. Collins

www.lindastrachan.com

First Published in paperback in Great Britain 2005

The rights of Linda Strachan and Sally J. Collins to be identified
as the author and illustrator of this work has been asserted by them
in accordance with the Copyright, Designs and Patents Act 1988

Design - Veneta Altham

Reprographics - GWP Graphics

Printing - Printer Trento, Italy

Published by

GW Publishing
PO Box 6091
Thatcham
Berks
RG19 8XZ

Tel +44 (0) 1635 268080

ISBN 09546701-9-1

Hamish McHaggis
and the
Ghost of Glamis

By Linda Strachan
Illustrated by Sally J. Collins

One dark winter's night the friends had settled down cosily in Hamish's Hoggle.

"I wish Jeannie was here," Angus moaned. "She usually tells the best stories. When will she be back?"

"Not until the spring," said Hamish. "She's gone to Africa for the winter. But I could read you a story if you like?"

"A scary story?" asked Angus.

"Oh, yes!" Rupert said, settling down to listen. "I love a good ghost story."

Hamish began to tell the story in a deep, scary voice.

"It was a dark and misty night…"

"**Woo!**" howled Angus, pretending to be a ghost. "That was a scary story. I could be a great Ghost Hunter."

Woo!
Woo!

"Did you know?" Hamish said, as he closed the story book. "My grandfather, Rory McHaggis, lives in Glamis Castle?"

"I read somewhere," said Rupert, "that it is supposed to be the most haunted castle in Scotland. It sounds like a grand place. I would love to go and see it."

"What a braw idea!" chuckled Hamish. "We could go and visit my Grandpappy. He knows all about ghosts."

They started collecting their ghost hunting equipment.

Angus took a torch and a magnifying glass. He also took his whistle. "This will chase away the ghosts if they come too close."

Rupert packed some of his books about ghosts and castles.

"I hear Glamis Castle has some very fine pictures inside."

Spooky Castle Tales

Scary Stories

GHOST TRAIN

Hamish started packing his picnic basket. "We don't want to get peckish on the way. Ghost hunting sounds like a hungry business."

He also packed a mirror and a ball of string, in case they got lost in the castle.

Off they went with the Whirry-Bang
chugging and clunking over every bump.
"Oh look!" said Hamish. "It's snowing."
"Great!" chirped Angus. "We can build a
snow-ghost. Look, Rupert, snow!"

Clunk!
chug!

Clunk!
chug!

Rupert was fast asleep, gently snoring in the back seat.

Angus nudged him. "Wake up, Rupert, you old sleepy head."

"What? Who?" Rupert blinked and opened his eyes wide. "I say, is that snow?"

It was dark by the time they arrived. The full
moon shone behind the castle and the deep,
crisp, snow sparkled in the moonlight.

"What an enormous castle," Angus whispered.
"Is this where your grandfather lives, Hamish?"

"Aye, and there he is waiting for us."

Rory McHaggis met them at the door of the castle. Holding his candle high to light the way, he led them through the rooms.

"This is where some folk say the ghost of the Grey Lady appears," he told them.

"Have you ever seen her?" Angus whispered.

"Michty me, Laddie. You're looking a wee bit peely wally!" Rory laughed. "Don't you worry yourself about the ghosts. If you don't bother them, they won't bother you."

Rupert looked confused. "Peely Wally?
Who's he?"

Hamish grinned. "Grandpappy just
thinks Angus looks a little pale."

wheee eeee eeeeh

Snug in their beds Hamish and Angus were
about to go to sleep when Hamish whispered,
"did you hear that?"

Angus gulped. "What do you think it is?"

Aphhheeewwwhhoooo

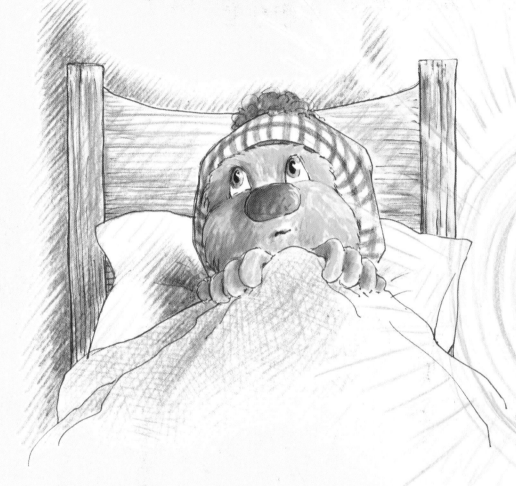

"There it goes again." Hamish sat up and grabbed
the bedcovers. "I think it's time to go ghost hunting,
don't you?" he said, jumping out of bed. He grabbed
one end of the ball of string and headed for the door.

Angus wasn't so sure, but he didn't want to be left
behind in the dark. "I'm coming, Hamish. Wait for me!"

wheee eeee eeeeh

"I think that scary noise is coming from up there," Hamish said in a wobbly whisper, pointing up the winding stone steps.

"It's getting louder," Angus whimpered.
"Do you think it's the ghost?"

Hamish stopped suddenly, making
Angus bump into him.

"Watch out!"

There was a large, dark shadow
coming down the stairs towards them.

"Aaargh!" yelled Hamish, as a huge shape came around the corner carrying a lamp.

"Hamish! What are you making all that noise for?" asked his grandfather.

"We heard noises and we thought you were a ghost!" Angus giggled, nervously.

"I was just coming to see what the noise was, myself," Rory McHaggis told them. "Never heard the likes of it in all my years at Glamis Castle. There it goes again. Come with me!"

The rumbling, whistling noise got louder and louder.

"It's coming from in here," said Rory, holding up his lamp.

The room was dark but the noise seemed to be coming from a large chair in the middle of the room.

"Is it the ghost?" whispered Angus, in a little, shaky voice.

Aphhheeewwwhhoooo o

Hamish wanted to run away but he also
wanted to see the ghost. The noise was
getting louder. Then it stopped for a moment.

They all stood still and waited.....

With a loud growl it started again.

Wheee eeeeh

They stepped closer
and closer...............

"That's no ghost!" Hamish laughed.

"What? Who? Where am I?" Rupert woke up with a start.

"You were snoring." Hamish told him. "It was a terrible noise!"

"And we thought it was a ghost!" Angus said, with a grin.

"I should have known!" laughed Rory McHaggis. "No self-respecting ghost would make a noise like that!"

At breakfast the next morning Rupert was snoozing noisily into his porridge.

"Can we come Ghost Hunting again, Mr McHaggis?" asked Angus.

"Of course," said Rory, giving the porridge another stir with his spurtle. "And bring your dozy friend, too. Looks like it might be time for him to coorie doon for his winter snooze."

"Come on, Rupert," said Hamish, gently shaking him awake. "It's time to go home."

"Goodbye, Grandpappy," said Hamish.

"Goodbye," said Rory. "Come back and see me again soon."

They all climbed back into the Whirry-Bang and headed home through the snow to Coorie Doon.

DID YOU KNOW?

Coorie Doon means to nestle or cosy down comfortably.

Blether means to gossip or chatter.

Peely wally means to look pale or sickly.

Braw means great or good.

Michty Me! is an exclamation.

Haggis. It is commonly thought that a Haggis has three legs, two long and one short. Hamish thinks this is very funny!

Angus is a Pine Marten.

Pine Martens can leap up to 12 ft through trees and branches.

Hedgehogs hibernate in the winter, sleeping for months at a time.

A Hedgehog nest is called a **hibernaculum**

Ospreys stay in Scotland from April until September, when they fly to Africa for the winter.

Glamis Castle was the childhood home of HM Queen Elizabeth the Queen Mother.

A **Spurtle** is a wooden stick for stirring porridge.

Hamish McHaggis and The Search for The Loch Ness Monster

Rupert doesn't believe in the Loch Ness Monster,
so Hamish and his friends take him to find Nessie.
09546701-5-9

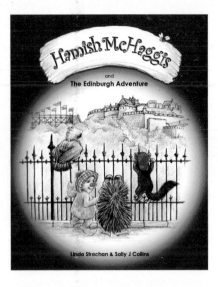

Hamish McHaggis and The Edinburgh Adventure

Hamish has tickets for the Tattoo at
Edinburgh Castle, but will they make it?
09546701-7-5

Hamish McHaggis and The Ghost of Glamis

Angus hears scary noises when they visit Hamish's
grandfather at Glamis Castle, could it be a ghost?
09546701-9-1

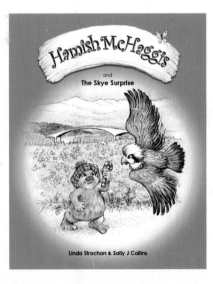

Hamish McHaggis and The Skye Surprise

Jeannie's brother is having a surprise party on the Isle
of Skye, but he's not the only one who gets a surprise.
09546701-8-3